DINOPANTS

To Mum, Dad, Laura and Ellie – C.M.

*To all the cavegirls and caveboys at
Hauxton Primary Cambridge – R.M.*

First published in Great Britain in 2009 by
Piccadilly Press,
A Templar/Bonnier publishing company
Deepdene Lodge, Deepdene Avenue,
Dorking, Surrey, RH5 4AT
www.piccadillypress.co.uk

Text © Ciaran Murtagh, 2009
Illustrations © Richard Morgan, 2009
Cover illustration by Garry Davies
Author photograph by Steve Ullathorne

ISBN: 978 1 84812 051 8

3 5 7 9 10 8 6 4

Printed in the UK by CPI Group (UK) Ltd, Croydon, CR0 4YY

DINOPANTS

Ciaran Murtagh

Illustrated by Richard Morgan

Piccadilly

CHAPTER 1

Charlie Flint ran round the corner and crouched behind a wall. The dinosaur was right behind him. His heart was pounding just as loudly as the dinosaur's footsteps. The ground was shaking and he could feel it juddering his bones. Charlie held his breath and counted to ten. The footsteps stopped and he breathed a sigh of relief. Maybe the dinosaur had realised that there wasn't much meat on a ten-year-old caveboy and had given up.

Charlie brushed his dark hair back off his forehead and decided to take a peek. Slowly, he put his hands on top of the wall and pulled himself to his knees. Bits of dust and rubble fell from the wall, covering his face and hair. Charlie gasped. The dinosaur was just a few metres away and it was still looking for him.

It was grinning like a maniac, its teeth glinting in the sunlight. Its nostrils flared as it sniffed the breeze, listening keenly, waiting for Charlie to give the game away. Charlie watched an enormous blob of dribble slither down one tooth and gloop on to the ground. Charlie gave a deep sigh and then realised what he'd

done. The dinosaur turned towards the noise. Charlie dropped back behind the wall and tried not to breathe. Had it seen him? The ground was trembling again and Charlie could hear the *THUMP, THUMP, THUMP* of dinosaur footsteps as they made their way through the mud towards him.

Charlie racked his brains. He had to do *something*. If he stayed there, the game was up, but where was he going to go? In front of him was a dead end and

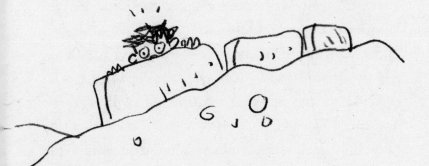

behind him was a dinosaur. The wall he was leaning on began to shake as the dinosaur got closer and closer. Particles of rock fell from the wall, bounced down Charlie's forehead and landed on his face. Charlie had that feeling you get when you're about to sneeze. He put his finger underneath his nose to stop the sneeze, but his finger was just as dusty as everything else. He couldn't help it – he absolutely had to sneeze! He took in a big gulp of air and then . . . and then . . . and then . . . the sneeze was gone.

Thank goodness! thought Charlie, and for one brilliant second, he was sure that everything was going to turn out fine.

'*ATCHOO!*'

The sneeze echoed down the road like thunder. The dinosaur stopped, narrowed his eyes and began to run straight towards him. Charlie heard the *THUMP, THUMP, THUMP* of enormous footsteps getting louder and louder until they stopped just the other side of the wall. Charlie could hear the dinosaur breathing, feel the breath on his neck over the top of the wall, even smell the stinking remains of whatever the dinosaur had eaten for lunch. Charlie tried to make himself as small as he could, but it was too late – the dinosaur eased up and looked over the wall.

Charlie saw his face reflected in the jet-black

eyeball of the green, scaly dinosaur. He shrieked and ran like he had never run before. He darted round the wall, through the dinosaur's legs and back down the road. He heard the dinosaur's teeth snap shut as it turned and lumbered after him. Charlie jumped over fences and dodged trees, sprinting past caves and stone buildings, his legs pumping, churning up clouds of dust behind him. But the dinosaur had him in his sights and he wasn't going to let him get away.

If I can just get to my cave, thought Charlie. *Just get in and shut the door.*

And there it was – Charlie's cave. Just at the end of the street. Charlie ran like his life depended on it, the dinosaur snapping at his heels. He reached his front garden and pushed at the gate.

It was shut. Charlie struggled, tugging it this way and that, but in his panic he couldn't open it. He looked behind him. The dinosaur was closing fast. Charlie tried to jump over the gate but it was too late. He felt the dinosaur's teeth grip him by his fur skin tunic and now he was flying through the air as the dinosaur tossed him high over his head.

'No!' cried Charlie as he somersaulted three times in the air. He watched the garden become the sky again and again and again and felt a little bit sick. Finally, he landed with a splat on the dinosaur's leathery tongue.

'Yuk!' cried Charlie as dinosaur slobber caked his hair and hands with thick green slime. 'That's disgusting!'

He looked into the dinosaur's cold, black eyes and laughed.

'All right, Steggy!' he giggled. 'You got me. That's two-one to you, but tomorrow you're hiding first.

And would it kill you to brush your teeth? What have you been eating?'

Steggy smiled and spat Charlie on to the ground, his tail wagging. Charlie picked himself up and dusted himself down.

'Would you look at yourself?' shouted Charlie's mother from the cave door. 'Do you know how long it takes to get those fur skins clean?'

Steggy put his tail between his legs and scuttled back to his kennel. He may have been a stegosaurus, but he was still a baby – a baby that was as tall as a house but a baby none the less – and even he was scared of Charlie's mum when she was angry.

'And you've torn the back of it!' yelled Charlie's mum. 'I can see your pants! I'll be up all night stitching that hole!'

'Sorry, Mum,' said Charlie, rearranging his fur skin so that his pants didn't show. 'It was only a game.'

'Well find a new one!' she ranted. 'My fingers are raw from scrubbing dinosaur spit out of your clothes. You won't be allowed to play with Steggy at all if you keep on like this!'

'Oh, Mum!' whined Charlie.

'Don't "Oh Mum!" me,' she snapped. 'Besides, it's disgusting. Who knows what's in that slimy spit of his?'

Charlie had heard it all before and switched off for a moment as his mum went on about this sickness and that sickness and what her sister had told her had happened to a little boy not far from there who liked to play games with dinosaurs.

'He was eaten whole!' she concluded. 'An accident of course, but still. And imagine what would happen if the Tyrannosaurus Rex decided to play? He wouldn't just pretend – he'd eat you up as soon as look at you, and then you'd be in trouble. And speaking of trouble, where's your club? Do you know how long your father and I saved to get you that?'

Charlie looked at his leather belt. His club should have been tucked into it. It was gone! It must have

fallen out when he crouched behind the wall.

'I'll go and get it, Mum. I know where it is,' he said,
opening the gate.

'Hang on a minute, young man!' called his mother.
'You're not going around the town covered in dinospit.
What will the neighbours say?'

But it was too late – Charlie was already out of the
gate and halfway down the road, dinospit or not.

CHAPTER 2

'What happened to you?' asked James Tusk, Charlie's best friend and sweet sharer, as he saw Charlie walking through town. 'You look like you've been swimming in a swamp!'

'It's Steggy's spit,' said Charlie. 'We were playing hide-and-seek.'

'Gross!' shouted James, pretending to be sick. 'You look like a walking, talking dino-bogey. If Natalie Honeysuckle could see you now!'

'So what if she could,' said Charlie. 'I don't care what she thinks!'

As far as Charlie was concerned, dinosaurs, clubs

and football were the most important things in life, and in that order.

James raised an eyebrow. 'Well, she cares what you think,' he said. 'Laura Shrub reckons she fancies you, and she's her best friend so she should know.'

Charlie blushed. 'Laura Shrub also thinks you can eat clouds if you get close enough,' he snapped. 'That doesn't mean she's right!'

'Whatever you say,' teased James. 'Here, stand still for a minute.'

James reached over and scooped some slime off Charlie's shoulder. Dabbing it on to his mousy brown hair and slicking it back he said, 'Much better. I find my hair all over the place in the summer months, don't you?'

Charlie raised his eyebrows and tried to remember which way he had run down the road. Was it left or right? It was always difficult to remember when you were being chased by a dinosaur. Deciding that it was from the right, Charlie headed off in that direction.

'Hey!' called James running after him. 'Wait for me! Why are you in such a hurry all of a sudden?'

'I left my club behind a wall while I was hiding from Steggy,' explained Charlie. 'I've got to find it or my dad will go mad.'

'Can he go more mad than he already is?' asked James.

'Look,' said Charlie turning to face his friend. 'Just because my dad's an inventor, that doesn't make him mad.'

'That's not what I heard,' said James, smirking.

'One day he'll invent something that'll wipe that smile right off your face,' said Charlie.

'Oh goody!' said James sarcastically. 'A smile wiper – just what the Stone Age needs!'

Charlie shot him a look.

'All right, all right, I'm sorry,' said James. 'How about I make it up to you by helping you look for your club?'

'Whatever,' said Charlie with a shrug.

As Charlie retraced his steps, James droned on and on to him about the adventures he'd had and the monsters he'd fought. Charlie knew it was all completely made up, but he didn't have the heart to tell James that. Besides, some of his stories were quite funny.

'Don't tell me,' boomed a voice from behind them. 'It's the one about the three-headed sea snake and the arrow of death.'

The voice belonged to Billy 'The Boulder' Blackfoot, the third member of their gang.

Charlie laughed and James smiled sheepishly.

'I was just getting to the good bit,' said James.

'James,' said Billy with a smile, 'with your stories there are no good bits.'

Charlie and Billy laughed. Billy's laugh was deep and gruff. He sounded and looked like a friendly giant. Even though he was just ten years old, he was already as tall as his dad and was showing no sign of stopping.

'What are you up to?' he asked.

'Looking for Charlie's club,' said James.

'Where did you last have it?' asked Billy.

'Just over there,' said Charlie pointing to the wall.

The three boys ran to the wall but the club was nowhere to be seen.

'Unlucky, Charlie,' said James.

'Someone must have taken it,' said Billy, shaking his head sadly.

Charlie's heart began to pound once more. He couldn't have lost his club. His parents would be so upset – it was made from the best hardened oak. Not only that, it was the one thing every caveboy needed. If you got into a scrape with a pterodactyl or had to beat a path through the jungle, then your club was what you wanted. He retraced his steps very carefully. He had ducked out from behind the wall just there. Charlie examined his scuffed footprints. And he had crouched beside that bit of weed, he remembered that. So where was his club?

'There's nothing here!' said Billy, kicking at the ground with a dirty foot.

'Nothing but this big pile of dinopoo,' said James, pointing at a gigantic, smelly pile of lumpy dinopoo just behind the wall.

'Looks like brontosaurus,' said Billy.

'How can you tell?' asked James.

'Well, it's almost as tall as me for one thing,' said Billy knowingly. 'And there are bits of twig and leaf in it. Bronties like twigs and leaves. And of course it's in the traditional half-moon shape so it's definitely a bronty-bottom poo. If you look at the texture . . .' Billy was about to go into even more detail – for some reason dinopoo was his favourite subject – when Charlie stopped him.

'Are the two of you going to help me look for my club?' he shouted. 'Or are you just going to stand there talking about dinosaur poo? I mean, how disgusting can you get? What's so interesting about dinopoo anyway? It's big and smelly and brown . . .'

'Some of it's green,' interrupted Billy.

'I don't care!' shouted Charlie. 'It's *everywhere*!'

And then he stopped. It *was* everywhere. But it hadn't been earlier on. He was sure he would have noticed a big pile of dinosaur poo behind the wall – he hadn't been *that* caught up in the game. And then it dawned on him . . .

'I know where my club is.'

'Oh good,' said James. 'Did you leave it in your bedroom?'

'No, it's not in my bedroom,' said Charlie quietly.

'Then where is it?' asked Billy.

Charlie looked towards the big brown brontybottom poo.

His friend's eyes widened and Charlie nodded.

'Yuk!' said Billy, backing away.

James was too busy laughing to say anything. When he finished laughing all he could say was, 'Charlie's got a poo club, Charlie's got a poo club,' over and over again.

'You've got to help me,' said Charlie.

'How?' Billy asked.

'Maybe we could lift it or something?' said Charlie desperately.

'No way!' James shouted. 'You're on your own for this one.'

'Fine,' said Charlie. 'I'll just have to do it myself.'

'Shouldn't that be "*poo* it yourself"?!' laughed James, but he soon stopped when Billy punched him on the arm.

The two boys looked at their unlucky friend.

'A caveboy's got to do what a caveboy's got to do,' said Billy with a grim nod.

Charlie gritted his teeth, clamped his hand over his nose and plunged his arm deep into the big brown poo. It felt disgusting – like running your hand over the edge of a squelchy swamp or sticking your arm into a bowl of lumpy custard. His fingers squirmed and stretched until they finally touched something hard.

His friends were pulling all sorts of faces. They looked like they were chewing a very nasty piece of liquorice.

'Have you got it?' asked James.

'I think so,' said Charlie. His fingers gripped around the object and with a *squelch*, a *slurp* and a *splat*, Charlie pulled it free.

He looked up to see his club, a little browner than before, sticking to his hand like glue. Charlie smiled a very forced smile.

Billy and James were jumping up and down, clapping and cheering.

'Well done, mate!' shouted James.

'Yeah, Charlie, that was very brave!' said Billy.

Charlie wiped his arm on some leaves, and then the three boys collapsed into fits of giggles.

Charlie promised to meet his two friends the next day for the walk to school and then headed for home.

His mum made him have a bath. She heated water over the fire and then poured it into the leaf-lined hole in the ground that his dad had dug for the purpose.

He dived straight in, taking his club with him, much to the annoyance of his mother. She didn't seem to notice the strange smell coming from her son, or if she did, she must have put it down to dinospit rather than something more disgusting.

As Charlie lay in bed that night, his clean club by his side, he heard his dad come back from work.

He hadn't invented anything in months and Charlie listened to his mum and dad talking when they thought he was asleep. If his dad didn't come up with a new invention soon then he was going to be fired.

Charlie didn't like to think about that and, as he closed his eyes, he hoped he would dream of an invention that might save his dad's job.

CHAPTER 3

Friday mornings were Charlie's worst time at school. The first lesson was hunting and Mrs Heavystep sent the class out to catch a sabre-toothed tiger. Billy was brilliant at hunting. He knew just the right time to chuck his spear and when to throw his vine net. Charlie watched in awe as he chased the tiger this way and that. James tried to keep out of the way – he didn't like anything that might dirty his expensive jaguar fur skin, especially not sabre-toothed tigers. After what seemed like hours, Billy finally caught the tiger and bonked it on the head with his club. He was given a flint spear as a reward, and then it was back inside for stone-shaping.

Stone-shaping was another boring lesson. You had to tap away at rocks for hours in order to make them sharp or a useful shape. By the end of the class, Charlie's hands were covered in tiny scratches where he had slipped and sharpened himself instead of the rock. By the time it got to cave painting, Charlie was dreaming of lunch-break and the game of football he was going to play with Billy and James.

When the sun shone on the red rock it was time for lunch. Mrs Heavystep told them to put down their tail-hair paintbrushes, to watch out for the T. Rex and to be back before the sun shone on the yellow rock. Then she marched off to the staff room.

The three boys picked up their bags and went to sit in the sunshine to watch the dinosaurs go by.

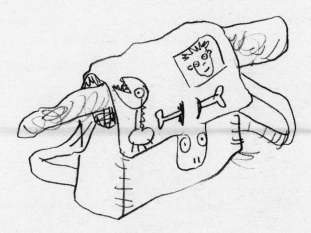

For the most part, dinosaurs and humans lived happily together in the town of Sabreton. Years ago they had decided it was silly to go about killing each other so they had called a truce. Everyone had agreed to it – everyone except the T. Rex. He still lived alone out on the mountain. But apart from him all the dinosaurs wandered around Sabreton happily, and Charlie and his friends loved to watch them go by.

'There's a velociraptor,' said Billy, pointing at a small dinosaur scurrying on two legs past the school gates.

'And there's a triceratops,' said James. 'They're my favourite.'

'Steggy's *my* favourite,' said Charlie, biting into the mammoth meat wrapped in vine leaves that his mum had made him.

'That looks delicious,' said James. 'I wish my mum made things like that.'

'Why?' asked Charlie. 'What have you got?'

James held up a handful of nettles and a clump of limp rhubarb. The other boys laughed.

'Laugh all you like,' said James, 'but I'm starving!' As if on cue his stomach rumbled loudly.

'Cripes!' said Billy. 'Was that you or thunder?'

James punched him on the arm.

'How about a game of football to take your mind off it?' said Charlie, finishing his food and bouncing his football on the ground.

'I don't know,' said James weakly. 'I don't think I've got the energy.'

'Don't be such a wimp!' said Billy, taking the football. 'You can be in goal.' Billy bounced the mammoth-hide ball off James's forehead.

'Hey!' shouted James. 'Watch my hair!'

'Why?' asked Billy. 'What's it going to do?'

The three boys packed away what remained of their lunch and ran towards the football pitch. Charlie put his bag by the goalpost and the other boys did the same.

'Three and in?' asked Billy.

'Sounds good to me,' said Charlie.

James kicked the ball down the field and Charlie ran after it.

Charlie was a fantastic footballer – he was quick and light on his feet but he also had power when it came to shooting for goal. He dribbled the ball back towards the goal, dodging the potholes and rocks that littered the bare-earth pitch. The ball moved like it was glued to his foot.

Billy, on the other hand, had no real skills when it came to football, but it didn't matter. He was so huge that he only had to stand in your way and you had a problem. Sometimes, if he was feeling really nasty, he would shoulder-barge you off the ball and you'd still be feeling it the following week.

Charlie ran towards his man-sized friend.

'Come on, Charlie!' shouted James from the goal. 'You can get past him! Look who's watching!' James nodded towards the edge of the pitch where Natalie

Honeysuckle was standing.

Charlie felt himself begin to blush. Then he remembered where he was and focused on the game.

'You'll never get past me!' said Billy. Charlie knew his friend was only joking but Billy was still quite scary, even when he was pretending. 'Come and have a go at the king of the hunters!' growled Billy beating his chest. Charlie's heart fluttered nervously. He could feel Natalie Honeysuckle's eyes following his every move.

Charlie lowered his head, squared his shoulders and ran towards the goal, weaving this way and that. Billy was just in front of him and was blocking his way with his size-twenty feet. With a quick flick, Charlie chipped the ball over the big boy's head and darted to the left. Billy didn't know whether to follow the ball or Charlie and before he knew it Charlie was past him and the ball was in the goal.

Charlie pulled his fur skin over his face and ran towards Billy in a lap of victory. His pink tummy, full of mammoth and vine leaves, jiggled as he ran. James, standing in the mouth of the goal, coughed to get his attention. Charlie quickly pulled down his fur skin and saw James pointing to where Natalie Honeysuckle was giggling and waving in their direction. Charlie felt his cheeks begin to burn.

'Cool,' said Billy, smiling. 'Very cool.'

'Do you show your tummy to all the girls?' asked James. 'Or just the ones you fancy?'

'Just kick the ball,' yelled Charlie, trying to ignore his blushes.

But before James had a chance to kick the ball anywhere, the ground began to shake.

'Is that your stomach again?' asked Billy.

James shook his head. 'Nothing to do with me this time.'

'Oh no,' said Charlie, his eyes wide.

'What is it?' asked Billy.

Charlie pointed towards the school. His two friends turned to look.

'Diplodocus!' screamed James.

It was huge. Bigger than huge, in fact – one of the biggest of all the dinosaurs. Its long neck towered high above the school and its whip-like tail swished back and forth knocking

over trees and boulders. It was heading straight for them.

Even though diplodocuses were huge, they weren't vicious like the T. Rex. They never ate anyone and they didn't have particularly sharp teeth. But they were stupid, which was dangerous enough – and, worse than that, they were very, very clumsy. Sometimes they forgot that they shared the earth with millions of other things much smaller than themselves and wandered through Sabreton causing havoc. Charlie watched its boulder-

sized feet march towards the football pitch.

'What's it doing here?' asked Billy, the shaking ground making his voice wobble. 'I thought the big dinosaurs were supposed to keep out of town.'

'Do you want to stay here and tell it that?' asked James as he steadied himself against a goal post.

'It's probably lost,' said Charlie, holding on to the goal post too. 'Come on! We've got to get out of the way.'

'What about Natalie?' asked Billy, pointing to the touchline.

Charlie looked. Natalie Honeysuckle was standing stuck to the spot in terror.

'Natalie!' he called. 'Get out of the way!'

Natalie looked up but didn't move. Clouds of dust were now surrounding the football pitch and the ground was shaking like an earthquake.

'You've got to get out of the way!' called Charlie, waving his hands frantically. But it was no use – Natalie couldn't see a way to escape. Billy and James ran for the safety of the school building but Charlie couldn't leave Natalie on her own.

The diplodocus was almost on top of them. One massive tree-trunk leg landed just beside Charlie, knocking him down and causing the ground around him to split open. He looked towards the sky and saw the stupid, vacant face of the diplodocus miles above him. It seemed to be humming.

'Hey!' he called, waving up at the dinosaur. 'Down here!'

But it was no use – the dinosaur couldn't hear him.

There was only one thing for it – Charlie would have to rescue Natalie himself. He looked across the football pitch. There might just be a way through. Charlie ran towards the girl. The dinosaur was right above them now and Charlie darted over the rumbling earth underneath its massive grey belly. Its feet were landing all around him, churning up the ground so that it looked more like the sea than solid earth. Using all of his footballing skills, Charlie was forced to weave and duck past flying boulders and gaping chasms until finally he was standing beside Natalie.

'Come on!' he said, grabbing her by the arm. 'We've got to go.' And using all of his strength, Charlie pulled the girl back across the football pitch.

Dodging back and forth past the swishing tail of the diplodocus, Charlie tried to imagine himself running towards a goal rather than away from a dinosaur's foot. Soon Charlie could hear the yells of his classmates calling him towards the safety of the school building. He dived through the doorway, dragging Natalie behind him, and Mrs Heavystep slammed the door shut after them.

The class waited in the stone schoolroom until the diplodocus passed.

The massive earthquake became tiny tremors until finally there was no shaking at all. Charlie received so many pats on the back that he lost count, and even Natalie managed to thank him when she finally got over her fright.

James and Billy gave him a thumbs-up.

'Right,' said Charlie when all the commotion had died down. 'Still another few minutes of lunch-break left. Who's for one last kickabout?'

'I'm not so sure about that,' said James.

'Why not?' asked Charlie. 'That dippy diplodocus has gone now. It won't be back.'

'Yeah,' said Billy, pointing out of the window. 'But it's left us a not-so-little present. Look.'

Charlie looked outside and his jaw dropped. There, on the football pitch, was the biggest pile of diplo-dung he had ever seen. There was no way they'd be playing on that pitch for a while.

'I don't believe it,' said Charlie, shaking his head.

'I know,' said Billy. 'Right on the penalty spot!'

'First my club and now this,' said Charlie. 'Something has got to be done.' And he vowed to be the person to solve the dinopoo problem once and for all.

CHAPTER 4

Charlie sat outside all afternoon crouched over a dry patch of earth with a stick. He had begun to sketch out ideas for getting rid of the dinopoo as soon as he got back from school earlier that afternoon. So far none of them had been successful. Dust clouds formed where he had started a diagram or a picture only to realise a problem with it halfway through. The earth in front of him was littered with crossed-out ideas and smudges. Charlie bit down on the end of his stick and thought even harder.

Steggy poked his head into the garden, hopeful for a game of hide-and-seek.

'Not now, Steggy,' said Charlie to his dinosaur friend. 'I've got to think.'

Steggy made a yelping, cooing sound and licked Charlie's face.

'No, Steggy!' said Charlie, batting the tongue away. 'I can't play now!'

Steggy opened his eyes as wide as he could and made his sweetest, cutest face. Charlie looked at him and shook his head.

'I've got to come up with something to stop the dinopoo,' he explained.

But Steggy didn't understand. The dinosaur sighed a big, deep, smelly sigh and lumbered back to his kennel.

'Sorry, Steggy!' called Charlie after him, but Steggy was too busy sulking to listen.

Charlie stared at the ground. All of his ideas were rubbish. No wonder his dad always looked so worried – it was a hard job being an inventor.

To begin with he'd started small. He'd got the idea from the jars standing on his mum's kitchen shelf. When you wanted to keep things inside a jar, you put a stopper in it, so why couldn't you do the same if you wanted to keep things inside a dinosaur? Excitedly Charlie had begun to sketch out the workings of a brand new contraption, one that would put stoppers into dinosaurs' bottoms and keep the stinky steggy-plops and bronty-bottom poos safe inside.

He'd got quite far with the idea when a few problems began to bother him: *What happens when they fart?* he thought. Stoppers would be flying out of dinosaurs' bottoms here, there and everywhere, and that could be dangerous. You'd be walking down the street when all of a sudden a dinosaur would let rip and before you knew it you would be shot at by a farty dino-bottom-stopper. *And even if we ignore the flying farty bottom-stopper,* thought Charlie, *even if we pretend that the cork could stay in a dinosaur's bottom for ever, what would happen to the dinoplops then? They couldn't stay inside, could they?* Before long there'd be massive, bloated dinosaurs walking up and down the street, full to the brim with bronty-bottom poos and stinky steggy-plops. Then they'd probably explode. Which would be even worse. Lots of little dinosaur time-bombs walking around the town just waiting to burst with big brown dino-dung.

So, Charlie thought, someone would have to pull the stoppers out every now and then in order to make sure the dinosaurs didn't explode. Who'd want that job? They'd probably give it to the person that had come up with the whole silly idea in the first place. And that was him. And there was no way he was going to spend the rest of his life pulling the stoppers out of dinosaurs' bottoms. He'd come up with the idea to get away from dinopoo, not to spend the rest of his life cleaning it up

at ridiculously close quarters.

So that idea had found itself scrubbed out, rather than causing him a lifetime of scrubbing, which all things considered, thought Charlie, was probably for the best.

And so it had gone on into the evening. He'd had

one idea involving string, one involving nettles and one terrible idea that had involved a monkey and a bucket. Dejected, Charlie kicked the ground angrily. *This is awful*, he thought, his head slumping in his hands. How hard could it be to come up with one good idea?

Charlie didn't hear his dad come back from work until the garden gate clicked.

'Tough day, son?' asked his father.

Charlie mumbled something into his folded arms.

'I know just how you feel,' said his dad pulling at his particularly disgusting leopard-skin tie and standing beside him. He looked at the drawn-on earth.

'These all yours?' he asked, pointing to the scratched out designs.

'Uh-huh,' said Charlie.

'What's the monkey for?' asked his dad examining a drawing.

'Don't ask,' Charlie replied.

'I see,' said his dad. 'That bad.'

'I'm trying to invent something,' blurted Charlie, 'something that will stop all the dinopoo. But my ideas are rubbish.'

'They're not rubbish,' said his dad, looking at another diagram. 'Some of these show a lot of imagination.'

'But they don't work!' whined Charlie.

'Sometimes,' said Charlie's dad wisely, 'it's just as important to know what won't work as what will. That way you don't waste your time.'

'I'm just not thinking hard enough,' moaned Charlie.

'Or maybe,' said his dad, 'you're thinking too hard. Sometimes the best ideas are the ones that come to you when you're least expecting it.'

Charlie didn't believe a word of it. He was used to his dad saying things like that just to make him feel better. He knew he was being stupid and that was that. There had to be a solution, he just wasn't clever enough to think of it.

'You look tired, son,' said his dad, tracing his fingers over the drawings. 'Why don't you go to bed and look at these in the morning. They may seem better with a fresh head.'

Charlie nodded. He was feeling very sleepy. Perhaps some rest would do him good. He gave his dad a goodnight kiss and headed for bed.

Charlie's father stayed a bit longer looking at all the drawings and diagrams. *A way to get rid of dinopoo,* he thought to himself shaking his head. How could Charlie possibly think he could do that? Sometimes he didn't understand children at all.

★ ★ ★

In his bedroom, Charlie untied his belt and hung it over a bed post. Then he leaned his club against the wall next to his bed in case he needed it in the night. His mind was still whirring as he pulled his fur skin over his head and dropped it to the floor. He knew that made his mum angry but he was suddenly feeling far too tired to pick it up. He pulled off his pants and clambered under the tiger skin sheets. As he lay there gazing up at the ceiling, letting himself nod off to sleep, an idea popped into his head. It was only a tiny idea, hardly an idea at all really. But as he closed his eyes that night, Charlie Flint knew he had just found the idea he had spent all afternoon looking for.

CHAPTER 5

'Dinopants!' said James, snorting milk out of his nose. 'What on earth are dinopants?'

'They're the answer to our nightmare!' said Charlie with a grin.

He was sitting in his front room the following Saturday. Billy and James sat cross-legged in front of him drinking cups of milk and Charlie had drawn a picture in the ground. He was pointing at it with a long stick.

'You see,' began Charlie, 'the problem is that the dinopoo just comes out and out and out. This diagram clearly shows that.'

Charlie pointed at a picture he had drawn of some dinopoo – lots of dinopoo in fact. James and Billy nodded nervously.

'Dinosaurs go whenever and wherever they feel like it,' explained Charlie, 'which is why our town is littered with stinky steggy-plop-plops and horrid bronty-bottom poos.'

'Don't forget the dirty diplo-dung,' said Billy.

'Yes,' agreed Charlie. 'Who could forget the dirty diplo-dung? What we need to do is to give them a reason to think twice before they . . .'

'Do their business?' offered James.

'Exactly,' said Charlie. 'And my dinopants will give them that reason.'

Charlie pointed his stick at a very crude drawing of a pair of massive Y-fronts. 'We just put the dinopants on to the dinosaur and hey presto!' Charlie pointed to another picture. 'No more dinopoo!'

Charlie had drawn a brontosaurus wearing the Y-fronts. His long tail popped out of a hole in the back. James and Billy looked at each other and then fell about laughing until it hurt.

'They look ridiculous!' giggled James. 'They'll never catch on!'

'What do you mean?' asked Charlie.

'You'll never get the dinosaurs to wear them, Charlie,' explained Billy. 'Dinosaurs don't wear pants.'

'They don't wear pants *yet!*' insisted Charlie.

'No,' said Billy. 'They don't wear pants *ever!*'

'Is this a joke?' asked James. 'Can we go and play football now?'

'It's not a joke,' said Charlie grumpily. 'And we can go and play football after the fashion show.'

'Fashion show?' gasped Billy.

'Steggy!' called Charlie. 'You can come in now!'

Steggy flounced into the room, ducked his head under the doorway and did a little pirouette in front of Charlie's picture. The two boys slowly put their milk on the floor and watched with open mouths. Steggy was wearing a pair of home-made frilly pink knickerbockers.

'You've gone completely mad,' said James.

'Stark raving bonkers,' agreed Billy.

'He loves them!' said Charlie proudly. 'I can't get them off him. Unless he wants to . . .'

'Steggy-plop-plop?' asked Billy.

'Exactly!' nodded Charlie. 'They're a pair of old bathroom curtains. It's amazing what you can pick up in skin-stitching classes, although I still haven't got used to the needle.'

Charlie showed the two boys his palms. They were covered in angry-looking scratches and scars. 'I was up half the night,' said Charlie. 'What do you think?'

'I think I don't know who's more mad,' said James. 'You or your dinosaur.'

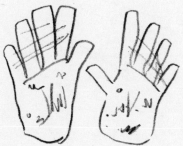

Steggy was really playing up to his audience. He was

flashing his teeth and had one arm placed behind his head. He shimmied around the living room making sure the boys got to see his new knickers in all their glory.

'People always think that inventors are mad,' said Charlie.

'Yes,' said James, 'but this time they'd be right. You really are mad! I mean – dinopants? It'll never work.'

'Steggy doesn't seem to agree with you,' said Charlie. 'Besides, you haven't seen all of them yet.'

'What do you mean, "*all* of them"?' asked Billy nervously.

'Like I said, I had a very busy night. Go and get changed, Steggy, and let's show them what we've got!'

With that Steggy swished his tail and was gone.

Over the next twenty minutes, Steggy came back into the living room wearing a different pair of

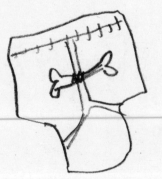 

dinopants every time. Some were frilly and some were spotty, some were furry and some were silky. On one particularly memorable occasion, Steggy came into the living room wearing a pair of disgusting green pants that had a mini Steggy embroidered across the bum in bright yellow. By the end of the display both boys sat with their heads in their hands.

'Well?' asked Charlie. 'What do you think?'

James looked at his friend and, for the first time in his life, he honestly didn't know what to say.

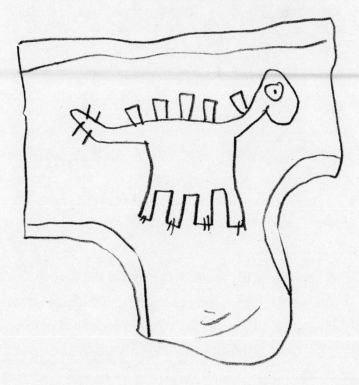

'I think,' said Billy very slowly indeed, 'that you need to go and have a very long lie down. You're obviously not feeling well.'

'Rubbish,' said Charlie with a smile. 'I've never felt better. And we haven't got time for a lie down – we've got a meeting with the Mayor in twenty minutes.'

'A meeting with the Mayor!' spluttered James.

'Yes,' said Charlie. 'I'm going to tell him all about my dinopants. If he agrees, there could be a pair on every dinosaur walking through Sabreton by the end of next week!'

'Oh dear,' said Billy shaking his head. 'Oh dear, oh dear, oh dear.'

CHAPTER 6

The Mayor of Sabreton's office was big and impressive. Hand-woven rugs of leaves and rushes lay strewn on the floor, some of the finest cave paintings the boys had ever seen were daubed across the walls, and a variety of animal skins covered the Mayor's chair and desk.

The three boys stood nervously waiting for the Mayor to arrive.

'You're sure about this?' whispered James to Charlie. 'We could still leave now and never talk about this whole silly idea again.'

'Nonsense!' said Charlie, his rolled-up dinopants popping out from underneath his arm. 'The Mayor is going to love my dinopants, just you wait and see!'

Billy and James exchanged nervous glances.

James looked at the door and wondered if he still had time to run before Charlie embarrassed them all and maybe got them kicked out of Sabreton for ever.

Billy sensed what he was thinking and gripped him by the shoulder. 'Don't you dare,' he hissed. 'We're *all* in this together.'

James rolled his eyes and stared at the ceiling.

Just then, the door swung open and the Mayor's bodyguard burst into the room. He was even taller than Billy and was wearing a lavish fur skin covered with badges and medals. He pulled a tiny wooden trumpet from his pocket and tooted a salute. As he finished his tooting, he bowed and the Mayor of Sabreton walked majestically into the office.

While his office was big and impressive, the Mayor was not. He was a lot shorter in real life than he looked on the cave paintings, and his face was round and dimpled like a squashed pink football. He had a moustache that bristled when he walked. A huge, shiny emerald dangled from a strip of leather round his neck and Charlie wondered how such a small man managed to wear it all day without either tripping over or toppling forward under its weight.

The Mayor peered up at the three boys. All were

taller than him. Billy was almost twice his size.

'Which one of you is Charlie?' asked the Mayor, looking at each of the boys in turn.

Charlie slowly raised his hand.

'So who are you?' The Mayor stared at Charlie's friends.

'My name's James Tusk,' said James, 'and can I just

say how pleased I am to meet you, Your Worshipfulness.'

The Mayor smiled.

'And can I also say,' said James with a bow, 'that absolutely none of this is my idea.'

Billy dug him in the ribs with an elbow and hissed at him to be quiet.

'And who are you?' asked the Mayor looking up at Billy.

'Billy Boulder, Sir,' said Billy.

'Well, Billy Boulder, play your cards right and one day you might be my bodyguard. What do you think of that, Boris?'

The Mayor looked over at his bodyguard who shuffled uncomfortably by the door. The Mayor laughed. 'Don't worry, Boris, you've got a few years yet. Now then, gentlemen, what can I do for you?'

The two boys nudged Charlie forward.

'I have an idea,' said Charlie proudly, 'that will change Sabreton for ever.'

'In that case,' said the Mayor, 'you had better sit down and tell me about it.'

The Mayor pointed to three chairs that had been placed in front of his desk and the boys sat down.

'Well, Mr Mayor,' began Charlie.

'Call me Leslie,' said the Mayor.

James sniggered. Billy punched him in the arm.

'Well, Leslie . . .' said Charlie.

James sniggered again. Billy punched him even harder.

'. . . For years, Sabreton has been full of dinosaurs. Some of them choose to live with us and some choose to roam free. Some like to be our pets and some prefer to live in the wild. They get on with their lives and we get on with ours, and that's always been fine – apart from one thing. The dinopoo.'

The Mayor shifted uncomfortably in his seat.

Charlie pointed out of the window at the huge piles he could see. 'You've got big poo, small poo, lumpy poo, brown poo, slimy poo —'

'Green poo,' interrupted Billy.

'Green poo,' agreed Charlie before continuing. 'Yellow poo, round poo —'

'All right! All right!' said the Mayor flapping his hands. 'I get the message!' He turned away from the window. 'Dinosaurs poo,' he said. 'Can we move on?'

'I wish we could,' said Charlie. 'But only yesterday our football pitch was covered by an enormous pile of diplo-dung, and the day before that my club was covered by a big brown bronty-bottom poo.'

Charlie thrust his club in the Mayor's face just to make his point. The Mayor recoiled slightly but nodded sympathetically.

'Well, I've had enough,' said Charlie, his voice getting louder. 'And so has everybody else. I'm fed up of having to dodge steaming piles of steggy-plop-plops every time I go to the shops.'

'Steggy-plop-plops?' asked the Mayor in confusion.

'Steggy-plop-plops,' said Charlie nodding.

'He means —' started James.

'I think the Mayor knows what Charlie means,'

interrupted Billy before James got them into even more trouble.

'Which is why I have come up with dinopants!' Charlie proudly unrolled a pair.

James wished the ground would open up and swallow him whole.

'Dinopants?' said the Mayor, his moustache bristling.

Charlie nodded and before anyone could stop him he was explaining all about his brilliant dinopants idea.

Twenty minutes later, Billy and James were squirming in their seats as Charlie finished. To his credit, thought James, the Mayor had at least listened to Charlie's ideas. James was expecting to be thrown out of the office as soon as Charlie showed the  Mayor the first pair of pants, but instead the Mayor had just nodded politely and smiled. Maybe that was something they taught you at Mayor School, James thought, just after the lesson on moustache bristling.

There was a pause as Charlie rolled up the pants and then the Mayor began to speak.

Right, thought James, here it comes . . .

But much to James's surprise the Mayor didn't shout at them, didn't order Boris to throw them out by their feet or banish them from Sabreton for ever. Instead, the Mayor cleared his throat, looked at Charlie and said, 'Well done, Charlie, that was a very good presentation, very good indeed.'

Billy and James couldn't believe their ears. The Mayor was clearly as bonkers as Charlie. Charlie smiled smugly as if to say, 'I told you so.'

'You've obviously given this very smelly problem

some serious thought, and you have come up with an interesting solution. It's true that the people of Sabreton are sick and tired of these . . .'

'Steggy-plop-plops?' offered Charlie.

'Steggy-plop-plops,' agreed the Mayor. 'But there is a problem with your idea . . .'

Here it comes, thought James. *Prepare to be chucked out by Boris.*

'And what is that?' asked Charlie.

'You see,' explained the Mayor, 'man and dinosaur have been living together in Sabreton for years, since long before you were born. But it wasn't always like that. Once upon a time we used to fight terribly. Eventually a truce was called. The deal was that we don't interfere with them and they don't interfere with us. They can come and be our pets if they want to or they can choose to wander around by themselves, it's up to them. And all the dinosaurs agreed to that —'

'All except the Tyrannosaurus Rex,' interrupted Billy.

'All except the Tyrannosaurus Rex,' said the Mayor, nodding. 'But Charlie, how would you like it if dinosaurs started telling *us* what to do? They could decide that us building a football pitch might interfere with their right to poo wherever they want to. We can't make them do something they don't want to do. It just wouldn't be right. And even if we did force them, it would just start the fighting all over again. So thank you for your time but —'

'But they *want* to wear them,' interrupted Charlie. 'My dinosaur, Steggy, loves his dinopants. Just look out of the window.'

The Mayor went to his window and looked outside.

Steggy waved his tail at the Mayor and did a little twirl in his pink frilly knickerbockers.

The Mayor waved back. But what was even more amazing than the dinosaur in pink frilly knickerbockers he had just seen outside his window were the thirty other dinosaurs standing around Steggy, looking admiringly at his pants. One triceratops even appeared to be trying to buy Steggy's dinopants off him with half a dozen eggs.

'Amazing!' said the Mayor turning back to face the boys. 'Absolutely amazing!'

Charlie smiled.

With that, the Mayor seemed to make up his mind and nodded to himself.

'Right, Charlie,' he said thumping his desk. 'This might just work. What can I do to help?'

By the end of their meeting, the Mayor had promised Charlie some precious stones from the town funds to buy animal skins and whatever else they needed, and a room in the back of his offices to set up a production line. Work was to start after school on Monday.

'Well I never,' said James shaking his head as they left the office. 'He agreed to it. He actually agreed to it.'

Charlie was grinning from ear to ear. 'On Monday afternoon we start production,' said Charlie. 'And if all goes well, my dad won't have to worry about his job ever again.'

'Here's hoping the dinosaurs like their dinopants,' said James.

'They will,' said Charlie confidently. 'Soon every dinosaur in Sabreton will be wearing a pair.'

'Even the T. Rex?' asked James.

Charlie's smile faded a little. He hadn't thought about the T. Rex.

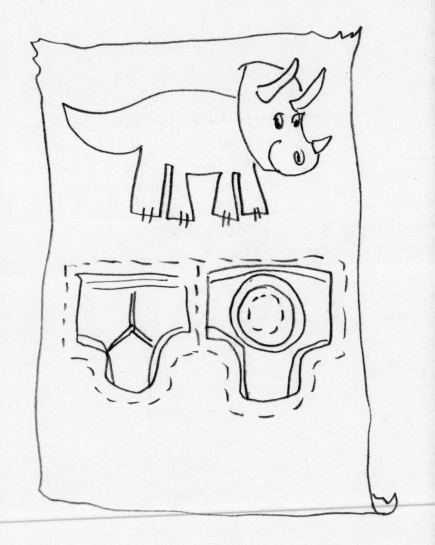

CHAPTER 7

On the Monday after the meeting, Charlie, James and Billy met after school in the room the Mayor had given them. It was filled from top to bottom with bits of animal hide. There were also three tables, three bone needles, and reels and reels of thread.

Before they began, Charlie showed his friends one of his designs. They were going to start with something small and easy — a simple pair of dinopants for a baby triceratops. Charlie showed them how to cut the skins and where to leave the holes for the tail and legs. He then asked them to make a pair each.

The results weren't brilliant. At one point Billy even

managed to stitch the pants to his fur skin. But by the end of that night his two friends had managed to make their first pair of dinopants. James put his on his head and danced around the room in triumph. It looked like so much fun that Charlie and Billy joined in and the three boys marched home happy, dinopants balanced proudly on their heads.

With practice, Billy and James were soon stitching dinopants as quickly as Charlie. This was just as well

because when they arrived at the room on Thursday afternoon, they found a queue of dinosaurs stretching down the street waiting for them to arrive.

'What do they want?' asked James.

'Dinopants!' said Charlie proudly, opening the door. 'It looks like our factory will have to be a shop too from now on.'

James stared at the queue. He'd never seen so many different types of dinosaur in the same place. They were all sorts of shapes and sizes, from thin iguanodons to big fat brachiosauruses with some triceratops, stegosauruses and even a brontosaurus thrown in for good measure. They all had something to trade – from precious stones to eggs, edible plants to the best quality flint – and they all wanted a pair of Charlie's dinopants.

'Right,' said Charlie to his friends. 'Looking at the queue, we've got a lot of work to do. I'll stay here and size them up, you two go in and dig out the dinopants we've made so far.'

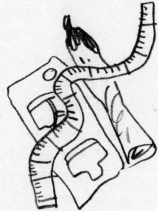

All that evening Charlie measured dinosaurs up for a pair of dinopants. If they had already made pants that fitted, then the dinosaurs

pulled them on there and then; if they didn't or if the dinosaur wanted something special, then Charlie made a note on the wall of the factory room and asked them to come back the following week.

By the end of the night, the boys had sold all the dinopants they had already made and had a list as long as Charlie's arm for new ones.

'We're going to need some help,' said James.

'Yeah,' agreed Billy, looking at the long list and shaking his head. 'My hands are already throbbing. There's no way we'll stitch that many pants by next week.'

'I've got an idea,' said Charlie.

'Oh no,' moaned James. 'Not another one!'

'Don't tell me,' sighed Billy. 'Dinosocks!'

Charlie laughed and punched him on the arm. 'An idea for making more dinopants, silly.'

The next morning, Charlie persuaded his dad to give up work for a day to help out at the dinopants shop instead. Then he managed to convince half his class to come and lend a hand later on, promising to pay them with sweets and sticks of liquorice. Even Natalie Honeysuckle spent a couple of hours stitching sparkly stones on to pink frilly knickers.

By the following Thursday there was a mountain of dinopants of all different shapes, sizes and colours piled

high in the corner of the room – there were furry tiger-striped pants, scaly crocodile-skin pants, and mammoth-hide ones dyed every colour from cherry red to blueberry. Charlie's dad decided not to go back to work at all and kept the shop open all day long, selling dinosaur after dinosaur a pair of Charlie's dinopants.

By the end of the week, every dinosaur in Sabreton was wearing them, and many were even coming back for a second pair. Some wanted snazzy stitching across the

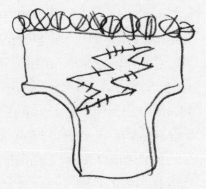

bum, some wanted pictures of themselves put on the back and some wanted pockets for storing snacks and leaves. Charlie stopped making the pants himself and became a dinopant designer, charging extra for one-to-one consultations and personalised designs.

Not only were they popular, but Charlie's idea was working brilliantly. There were hardly any bronty-bottom poos or steggy-plop-plops to be found in the whole of Sabreton. The Mayor set up a special field just outside the town where dinosaurs could go and do

their business whenever they wanted to, and all of them used it daily. Even the dippy diplodocus got the hang of it. The dinosaurs were so proud of their new pants that they didn't want anything to dirty them. They were forced to think before they pooed, and when they stopped to think they remembered the field and trotted off to use it.

It was going so well that Charlie's dad didn't have to go back to work if he didn't want to and Charlie's mum had plenty of things to trade for new fur skins.

The Mayor had even given them their own building to use as a factory and shop.

What was more, it didn't look like the work was going to dry up any time soon. Word had spread and dinosaurs were coming from far and wide to Sabreton just to buy a pair of Charlie's dinopants. Steggy was on hand to be fashion advisor and model. He tried on all the new designs and gave his approval. There was even a drawing of Steggy, wearing the frilly knickerbockers, painted on the outside of the shop.

'Well, Charlie,' said his dad one evening in the shop. 'It looks like your dinopants are making us a fortune.'

'We all thought he was mad, Mr Flint,' said James as he gift-wrapped a pair of lime-green boxer shorts for a grateful iguanodon. 'But just look at that!' James pointed to the line of patient dinosaurs stretching right out of town.

'And best of all,' said Billy, 'no more dinopoo.'

Charlie smiled a very satisfied smile: things couldn't get any better. And he was right. They were about to get a lot, lot worse.

CHAPTER 8

It was Billy who heard it first: a strange screeching roar that rang through the sky above Sabreton. He put down his flint knife and looked out of the window. 'What was that?' he asked.

Charlie and James turned to each other and shrugged. Then the screech-roar came again and Charlie's dad turned as white as a sheet.

'What's the matter, Dad?' asked Charlie.

'T . . .T . . .' he stuttered.

'Tea?' said James to Billy. 'He wants a cup of tea?'

'No, not tea,' spluttered Charlie's father, his eyes wide with terror. 'T. Rex!'

The boys had never heard the cry of a T. Rex before. The fighting between man and dinosaur had stopped long before they were born. The T. Rex had sulked off to the mountain and hadn't put a claw inside Sabreton since. But Charlie's dad was old enough to remember those terrible days. He may only have been a boy himself when he last heard that blood-curdling sound, but the cry of a T. Rex was never forgotten.

The dinosaurs by the shop heard it too and were looking nervously around them. There was another terrifying cry, part lion's growl and part raven's squawk. It was getting nearer – and suddenly everything went wrong. The dinosaurs who had, just five seconds before, been standing in a queue for a pair of dinopants, were frantically scrabbling to get away, shoving and biting each other in a desperate attempt to leave.

'Come on, boys!' said Charlie's father watching the chaos. 'We have to go too!'

'Go where?' asked Charlie.

'Anywhere!' shouted his dad. 'If we stay here we're going to be a T. Rex's supper!'

The three boys didn't need to be told again. Leaving their knives, needles and skins on the table, they ran towards the door. Charlie's dad pulled them down the street. They darted past the Mayor, who was desperately trying to calm down a herd of stampeding stegosauruses. The cry of the T. Rex rang through Sabreton once more and then even the Mayor began to run.

'Charlie!' he shouted as he ran, 'this way! There's a secret underground room left over from the fighting. We can hide in there!'

The Mayor pointed towards the town hall and the three boys, closely followed by Charlie's father, darted across the square to a trap door set into the ground just outside the town hall's front door.

'We can hide down here,' wheezed the Mayor as he pulled on a huge rope handle. 'It should be safe.'

Charlie's dad gave the Mayor a hand and the trapdoor creaked open. All around them dinosaurs were running to get away from the T. Rex. Buildings were being knocked over by tails and people were running around in the chaos, desperately seeking whatever safe place they could find.

'This is terrible,' said Charlie. 'What's the T. Rex doing in Sabreton?'

'I have no idea,' said the Mayor. 'But he doesn't sound happy!'

As if to emphasise the point, an ear splitting cry came from the far corner of the town square and Charlie turned to see the most terrifying dinosaur he had ever seen silhouetted against the evening sun.

'The T. Rex!' said Billy in disbelief.

'I hoped I'd never see another in my lifetime,' said

Charlie's dad, gazing up at the terrifying dinosaur.

The T. Rex made all the other dinosaurs look like teddy bears. There was evil in its eyes and blood on its razor teeth. Its tail lashed this way and that, upending trees and sending smaller, weaker dinosaurs skidding across the ground.

'Come on!' yelled the Mayor. 'There's no time to lose.'

Charlie's dad pushed the three boys down the carved stone steps that led from the trapdoor. Then he and the Mayor pulled the wooden door shut behind them as they hurtled down the steps themselves.

It was eerily quiet in the underground bunker. The Mayor produced a sparking flint from his pocket and lit the four torches that jutted out from the cold stone walls.

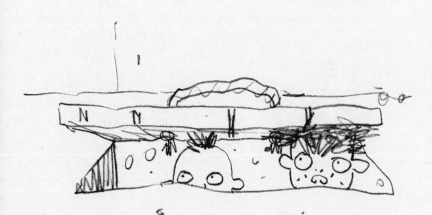

'I hoped I'd never have to use this place again,' said the Mayor shaking his head sadly.

'What's the T. Rex doing here?' asked Billy.

'If only there was some way of knowing what's going on,' said Charlie.

'Come with me,' said the Mayor.

He led them all down a corridor to a second underground room. Daylight streaked across an old wooden desk from a tiny window set high into the far wall.

'We can peep out here,' said the Mayor. 'It'll give us a clear view of the town square.'

Charlie put his eyes to the window and watched. The T. Rex was standing in the middle of the square howling his horrific cry into the evening sky. The dinosaurs that hadn't managed to escape stood cowering under his glare, trying not to move,

desperate not to
draw attention to
themselves. The
T. Rex let out yet
another deafening
roar and then slowly
the dinosaurs moved
towards him.

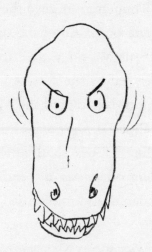

One by one, they
filed into the square,
eyes filled with
terrified respect. Within minutes the town square was
full of dinosaurs. Charlie didn't realise Sabreton had so
many dinosaurs in it. Just as he thought he'd seen every
dinosaur there was to see, Steggy walked sheepishly
into the square. Every single one of the dinosaurs was
wearing a pair of his dinopants. Every one, that was,
except for the T. Rex, who glared at the other
dinosaurs with his beady black eyes.

'What's going on, Charlie?' asked James in a
whisper.

'It's the T. Rex,' whispered Charlie back. 'He's
calling all of the dinosaurs into the town square. It
looks like they're having a meeting or something.'

'Oh no,' said the Mayor. 'It's a gathering.'

'A gathering?' asked James.

'They used to have them before a battle,' explained Charlie's dad. 'All of the dinosaurs, no matter how big or small, would gather to discuss tactics. They were always led by the T. Rex.'

'This is bad,' said the Mayor shaking his head. 'Very bad indeed.'

The T. Rex scoured the crowd of dinosaurs as if ticking off guests at a gruesome birthday party. Once he was sure everyone was accounted for, he began to talk to them in a series of low rumbles and shrill squawks. He was clearly very angry about something. As he roared and growled, the other dinosaurs looked

shame-facedly at the floor. After what felt like hours, the T. Rex let out one last, massive roar and glared at the dinosaurs.

After a moment, a triceratops walked slowly to the centre of the square, took off his dinopants and placed them at the foot of the T. Rex. Before long another three triceratopses and a brontosaurus had done the same.

'What's happening?' asked the Mayor.

'The dinosaurs are taking off their dinopants,' said Charlie sadly. 'They're just leaving them in the middle of the square.'

'Oh dear,' said the Mayor shaking his head. 'I was afraid something like this might happen.'

'What do you mean?' asked Charlie's dad.

'I think the T. Rex is angry at the other dinosaurs,' explained the Mayor.

'It certainly looks that way,' said Charlie. 'But why

are they throwing away my dinopants?'

'Do you remember what I said about the T. Rex refusing to accept the truce that was called between dinosaur and human?' asked the Mayor.

Everyone in the bunker nodded. They had all heard the story before.

'Well,' continued the Mayor, 'I think the T. Rex is angry at the other dinosaurs for wearing the dinopants. In his eyes, it's a step too far. He was happy for them to live with humans if they wanted to, so long as he didn't have to himself. But now they're wearing dinopants it's almost like they're embarrassed to be dinosaurs altogether and want to be humans instead. I think that's got him angry. Very angry indeed.'

Charlie looked out of the window. There was now a large heap of dinopants at the foot of the T. Rex and it was getting bigger by the second.

'But that's not what I meant to happen,' said Charlie shaking his head. 'That's not what I meant to happen at all! I just wanted the poo to go away. They're still dinosaurs.'

'I know that,' said the Mayor, patting Charlie on the shoulder. 'I think most of the other dinosaurs know that too. But when the biggest and scariest dinosaur of them all tells you to do something, then sometimes you just have to do it.'

Charlie looked sadly at the ever-increasing number of dinopants piled high in front of the T. Rex. Soon there was only one dinosaur left in the square wearing them. The T. Rex stomped towards Steggy and roared at him. Steggy looked up and slowly pulled off his dinopants. Charlie felt a tear roll down his cheek. After an agonising pause, the T. Rex took one long lingering look around the square, shook his head, roared and stormed off the way he had come.

The other dinosaurs watched him go, and slowly the dust settled.

'I think he's gone,' said Charlie, and they made their way slowly back up the cold stone stairs.

When they reached the town square, Charlie picked up Steggy's pair of pants from the pile and turned it over in his hands.

'I think this might be the end of dinopants,' said the Mayor sadly.

'Back to work for me then,' said Charlie's dad with a sigh. 'I hope Mr Crunch will give me my old job back.'

'It was fun while it lasted,' said James.

'Come on, Charlie,' said Billy, patting his friend on the back. 'Let's go and close up the shop. Maybe afterwards we can have a game of football to cheer ourselves up.'

'No,' said Charlie defiantly.

'What?' said James.

'No,' said Charlie again, a little louder this time. 'It's not over yet.'

'Charlie,' said Billy, 'you can't argue with a T. Rex. Besides none of the dinosaurs want to wear dinopants any more. Look.' Billy nodded towards the huge pile.

'They do,' said Charlie. 'They're just being bullied into throwing them away, and that's not fair.'

'Well, what can you do?' said James brushing cobwebs out of his hair.

'I can go and see the T. Rex,' said Charlie, staring at the mountain on the horizon.

James laughed. 'Sorry, Charlie, I must have spiders in my ears. I could have sworn you just said you were going to go and see the T. Rex.'

'I did,' said Charlie, gripping his club. 'I'm going tomorrow morning.'

And with that Charlie marched out of the town square and headed for home before his startled friends and worried father could do or say anything about it.

CHAPTER 9

'This time you really have gone mad,' said James the following morning, as he watched Charlie march purposefully around his bedroom stuffing clothes and sweets into a battered leather bag.

'You said I was mad when I thought up dinopants,' said Charlie, 'and look what happened there.'

'Dinopants were never going to eat you,' said Billy from a chair in the corner.

'The T. Rex might not eat me,' said Charlie bravely, but he didn't sound convinced.

Billy and James exchanged a look. Ever since Charlie said he was going to see the T. Rex they had been worried about their friend. They were a gang and they stuck together, but this T. Rex business sounded like suicide. They couldn't let Charlie do it. It was time for someone to take charge. Billy cleared his throat and stood up.

'Charlie,' he said, 'James and I have been talking . . .'

'Oh yes?' said Charlie picking up a spare fur skin and shoving it in his bag.

'We can't let you go.'

Charlie stopped his packing and looked at Billy.

'You know we'll always stand by you,' said Billy. 'James may be a bit of a wally sometimes —'

'Hey!' shouted James.

'And I can be a bit fierce on the football pitch.'

'Too true!' muttered James under his breath.

'But you're our mate and we can't let you do this.'

'It's too late,' said Charlie firmly. 'My mind's made up.'

'Come on, Charlie,' pleaded James. 'We've put up with a lot of your silly ideas in the past. My hands are raw from stitching dinopants for heaven's sake! But this is the silliest of the lot.'

'No, it's not,' said Charlie.

He looked at his two friends. James was all primrose scent and mint leaves and Billy was the gentle giant with the heart of gold. He had to make them understand.

'This isn't silly at all,' he explained. 'This is the most

serious thing I've ever done. It's not just about dinopants, not any more. We can't let a bully – and that's what the T. Rex is – ruin everything. The other dinosaurs are scared of him. All the people of Sabreton are scared of him. Even the Mayor is scared of him. *I'm* definitely scared of him, but something has to be done.

For a couple of weeks, everything in Sabreton smelled of roses rather than dinopoo and I want to live in that kind of town, not one that hides under the town hall every time the T. Rex decides to come down from the mountain.'

Billy looked at James. They could see that Charlie meant every word he said. Billy also knew that there was nothing anyone could say to stop

Charlie – he had that look in his eye, the one he'd had when he'd been talking to the Mayor and the one he'd had when he decided to help save Natalie Honeysuckle. There was something about Charlie Flint. You knew that when he made his mind up to do something, he was going to do it no matter what anyone said.

'Fine,' said Billy. 'Then we're coming with you.'

James nearly fainted. 'What!' he spluttered. 'Have you gone insane? Dinopants are one thing but T. Rexes are a very different, scarier and meaner matter.'

'James,' said Billy, 'we're his best friends. We can't just let him go up that mountain on his own.'

'I think you'll find we can!' squeaked James. 'If Charlie here

is stupid enough to go trotting up to a T. Rex's lair then
that's fine, but it doesn't mean I have to go with him.'

Billy fixed James with a meaningful stare.

'Don't stare at me like that,' said James. 'It's not
going to work!'

'Relax, you two!' chuckled Charlie. 'I don't want
you to come with me anyway.'

'See?' said James to Billy.

'But we want to come,' said Billy.

'Speak for yourself!' shouted James. 'I want to see
my eleventh birthday!'

Charlie laughed again. 'Billy,' he said, 'it's very kind

and brave of you to offer but I can't let you to do that.'

'See,' hissed James. 'He doesn't even want us to go, so stop offering before he changes his mind.'

'I'll come,' said Billy. 'We'll leave James behind.'

'Charming!' said James.

'No,' said Charlie firmly. 'I've got to do this on my own. It was my dinopants that made him angry, it's me that needs to sort it out. Besides, if I go up there on my own, maybe the T. Rex won't see me as a threat. We can just chat.'

'Just chat!' spluttered James. 'With a T. Rex! Maybe you can make him some teacakes and do a bit of cleaning while you're at it! You've really flipped this time, Charlie Flint, no two ways about it!'

'I'll be fine,' said Charlie, closing his bag and picking up his club.

'You'll be dinopoo by teatime!' said James.

Billy punched him on the arm.

'I'll be back before you know it,'

said Charlie giving each of them a slap on the back.

'What are your mum and dad going to say?' asked Billy.

'They're not going to say anything,' said Charlie, 'because they're not going to know about it. I'm climbing out through the window.'

'What?' gasped James. 'What if they ask us where you are? I'm not lying to them.'

'You don't have to. Just make sure they don't find out until it's too late for them to do anything about it. Stay in my room for an hour or so. They'll think I'm still in here playing. Then you can go out, and if they ask you, you can tell them.'

James looked at Billy, who was biting his lip.

'OK,' said Billy. 'We'll cover for you – but just this once!'

'Thank you,' said Charlie with a smile. 'I knew I could rely on you. I'll see you soon.'

Charlie slung his bag over his shoulder and climbed out of the window.

'Remember!' called Billy after him. 'Duck, swivel and find a way to bonk him on the head if things get scary!'

Charlie turned to see Billy demonstrating his famous sabre-toothed tiger take-down from hunting lessons through the window. Charlie laughed, waved

and then turned back towards the mountain.

'Well,' he said to himself quietly as he walked, 'you're all alone now, Charlie Flint. What have you got yourself into this time?' As he marched steadily towards the mountain, he allowed his brave smile to fade for the first time that day.

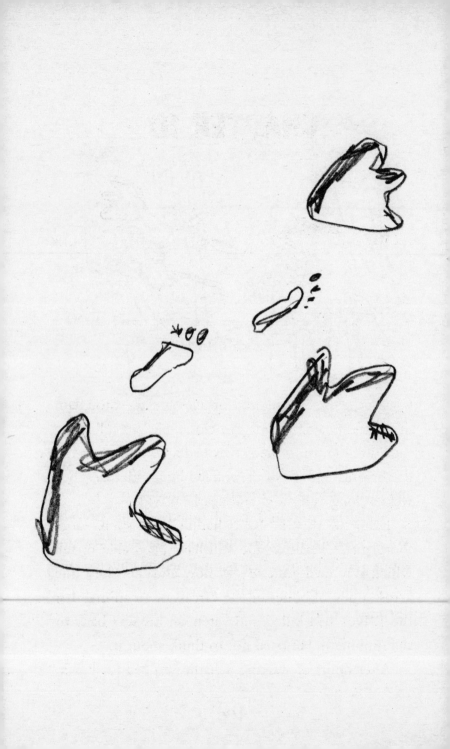

CHAPTER 10

Charlie had been walking for ages but the mountain didn't seem to be getting any closer. He was following the dusty footprints the T. Rex had left in the earth the day before. The size of them filled him with fear. They were as long as his arm and nearly as wide.

Even if the T. Rex hadn't left such large footprints, Charlie would still have been able to tell which way he'd gone. Every now and then he came across a pile of bones or the carcass of an animal that the T. Rex had killed and eaten on his way back to the mountain. He tried not to think about it.

After hours of walking, Charlie stopped for lunch.

He sat down on a rock and took a vine-leaf wrap from his bag. As he chewed, he looked back the way he had come. He could see the town of Sabreton nestling on the horizon. It looked so peaceful, and for a moment Charlie wished he could just click his fingers and magic himself back to his bedroom. Why did he always have to mess things up? Why did it always have to be him who came up with the big idea or the dangerous adventure? Would anyone blame him if he just picked up his bag and began the long walk back to Sabreton? He'd be home by teatime. He could tell them that he hadn't been able to find the T. Rex – they would never know.

Charlie gulped down the last piece of mammoth meat wrap and shook the thought from his head. He was Charlie Flint and one way or another he was going to sort this out. He had to stand up to the T. Rex, although he had no idea how – he didn't even know if the T. Rex would let him open his mouth before eating him whole, but he was about to find out. Charlie looked up at the mountain. *It's not that scary*, he thought, *it's only a mountain*.

A shrill cry filled the air. It was so loud that Charlie was sure he would be deaf for a week. It was a cry somewhere between a lion's roar and a raven's squawk – it was the cry of a T. Rex. Charlie froze and his blood ran cold. Once the cry died down, Charlie shook his head as if getting sand out of his ears. He looked up at the mountain. Grey clouds swirled menacingly around the peak, so that he couldn't see the top. He gritted his teeth, pulled his bag over his shoulder and put one foot on the path that led up the mountain. He paused to look behind him.

In Sabreton, smoke curled from chimneys and the sun shone on caves. He looked at his footprints. They stretched back as far as the eye could see. Next to them were another set, the set belonging to the T. Rex. They were huge by comparison! Charlie shuddered and continued on his way.

Charlie had been walking up the mountain for hours and the sun was setting behind him. He wasn't sure but he thought he had to be near the top now. The first bit of the mountain had been easy – there had been a path to follow and every now and then Charlie had walked past an upturned tree or claw-scuffed rock that told

him he was heading in the right direction. It was when he walked into the clouds that things got confusing. It was like walking in a thick fog. The path had disappeared and he could barely see his hand in front of his face. Now he was lost. He thought he might have been walking in circles. He had just passed a tree stump that looked just like the tree stump he had passed a while before.

Charlie slumped to the ground, put his head in his hands and began to cry. He felt very lonely indeed. He hadn't seen a single living creature – not so much as a bird or a mouse – since he'd started climbing. All the other creatures that roamed the earth were wise

enough to keep away from a mountain with a T. Rex on it. There was no sound, no movement, nothing. The only thing that let him know he wasn't entirely alone was the occasional ear-splitting cry from the T. Rex. It seemed to be getting closer and closer every time.

As if on cue, the T. Rex let out another shriek and Charlie shuddered.

He tried to stifle his tears but it was too much. He was lost in the clouds up a mountain. He was all alone and it was getting dark and somewhere out there was a T. Rex. Things couldn't get any worse. Charlie was smart enough not to cry as loudly as he wanted to because he didn't want to alert the T. Rex to his presence, but as he sat with his head in his hands, Charlie silently sobbed and shuddered with as much sorrow as he had ever felt in his young life.

Just then, something rustled in the bushes behind him. Charlie froze. Was this it? Was this the end? Had the T. Rex crept up on him? Charlie stopped sobbing and listened. He heard the deep rhythmic breathing of the T. Rex. He felt its breath on his face, gently ruffling his dark brown hair. Did it know he was here? Slowly and silently Charlie picked himself up. The leaves of the bush were rustling again. The T. Rex was getting closer and closer. Any minute now its terrifying head would emerge from the gloom, he would see its teeth flash and then he would be gone. *Well*, thought Charlie, *I'm not going without a fight*. He tugged his club out of his belt and held it high above his head.

'Come on, T. Rex,' he hissed though clenched teeth, his club gripped tightly in his hands. 'Let's see what you're made of.'

Slowly a green and scaly foot emerged from the bush. Almost immediately a second one appeared. Charlie didn't stop to think about himself, or the danger – with a mighty roar he leaped into the bush swinging his club as fiercely and ferociously as he could.

Leaves and brambles scratched his face as his club connected with thick dinosaur skin. He heard the breath fly from the dinosaur's lungs and smelled the fetid breath of the T. Rex. He swung again, aiming for where he thought the T. Rex's stomach would be, but instead of hitting stomach he felt his club connect with a head. This wasn't right, thought Charlie. The T. Rex was *much* taller than this. The dinosaur whined as Charlie took another swing, knocking it to the ground.

And now he was on top of it. He raised his club high, ready to do one of Billy's famous sabre-toothed tiger take-downs, but then he caught sight of the dinosaur's face. It was terrified! Its eyes were squeezed shut and it was bracing itself for another smack from Charlie's club.

'Steggy?' said Charlie in disbelief.

Steggy opened one eye and looked at Charlie.

'Steggy!' shouted Charlie hugging his friend with all his might. 'You stupid, stupid dinosaur! I thought you were the T. Rex!'

Charlie put down his club and pushed Steggy to his feet.

'What are you doing here?' he asked. 'I could have killed you.'

Steggy covered his face in a flurry of ticklish licks. Charlie laughed. It was then that Charlie noticed something else about Steggy. He was wearing dinopants.

'My dinopants!' said Charlie. 'You've put them back on.'

Steggy smiled a sheepish grin and Charlie smothered him in a cuddle.

'You came all this way to help me,' said Charlie. 'You're the bravest, most stupid dinosaur I know, but I wouldn't be without you for the world.'

Steggy gave him another lick.

'Right. It looks like the two of us have a T. Rex to find!' And filled with fresh confidence, Charlie stood

shoulder to shoulder with Steggy and together they
marched bravely into the clouds.

CHAPTER 11

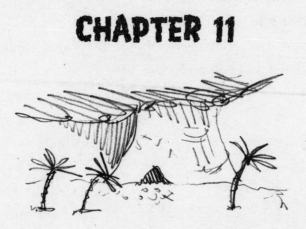

It didn't take them long to find their way back to the path. Steggy had a powerful nose and could smell the T. Rex and his lair in the distance. Following Steggy's lead, Charlie didn't feel half as lonely as he had done before and while he wasn't exactly cheerful, he wasn't upset any more either.

'Just so you know,' said Charlie, 'I wasn't scared up here on my own.'

Steggy made a noise that sounded like a laugh.

'I wasn't!' protested Charlie. 'But it's a good job you arrived when you did . . .'

Steggy smiled.

'. . . I needed someone to carry my bag.'

Charlie laughed and looped the bag over Steggy's neck. Steggy grumbled playfully.

Now that they were out of the clouds, Charlie could see how quickly the sun was setting. It was low on the horizon and bathed the entire valley in a golden glow.

'I hope we meet the T. Rex soon,' said Charlie. 'I want to finish this one way or another. If there's one thing more scary than being eaten by a T. Rex, it's being eaten by a T. Rex in the middle of the night.'

Steggy snorted in agreement.

They were walking across a long flat piece of ground. It was covered with pebbles and rocks and stretched a few hundred metres into the distance. The T. Rex had to be up here somewhere, thought Charlie – there was nowhere else for it to be.

The clouds swirled below them, and on one side of

the mountain was a sharp cliff. Charlie picked up a rock and dropped it over the edge. Although Charlie stood listening for nearly a minute, he didn't hear it hit the ground.

'It's a long way down,' said Charlie turning back to Steggy. 'Steggy? Are you all right?'

Steggy was standing frozen to the spot, sniffing the air.

'What is it?'

Steggy didn't answer, he just stared straight ahead. It didn't take Charlie long to see what Steggy was staring at. Ahead of them, before the edge of the mountain and the sky that followed, was a clump of trees and next to them was a cave that stretched deep into the belly of the mountain. It looked to Charlie like a

giant mouth open in a scream. 'The T. Rex's lair,' said Charlie in a hushed whisper. 'It's got to be.'

Steggy nodded, and slowly the pair made their way towards the cave. Charlie felt sure that their footsteps or scent would bring the monster out, but they managed to get all the way to the clump of trees without so much as a peep from the cave mouth.

It was a dark, horrible place. *Just the sort of place a T. Rex would live*, thought Charlie. Bits of slimy green vines hung from the cave mouth like witch's hair and piles of bones lay heaped on the ground. The remains of a hundred dinners that only the T. Rex had enjoyed littered the mountainside and a disgusting smell of half rotten meat and mouldy eggs filled the air. The smell made Charlie cough and splutter. He felt sure he would be tasting it for days to come – if he lived that long.

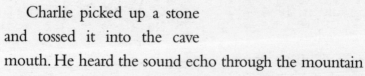

'Well,' said Charlie, 'this is it. Let's see if he's in.'

Charlie picked up a stone and tossed it into the cave mouth. He heard the sound echo through the mountain and held his breath waiting for the T. Rex to appear.

Nothing came.

Shrugging his shoulders, Charlie picked up another stone, larger this time, and crept a little closer to the cave. Steggy growled a warning but Charlie waved him away. Charlie threw the rock. It bounced off the cave wall with a thud but still there was no sign of the T. Rex.

Charlie bent down to pick up the largest stone he could find. Steggy growled and shook his head.

'Don't worry,' hissed Charlie, 'I don't think he's in.'

A roar erupted from the cave like a clap of thunder. Charlie dropped the stone in terror. Dust billowed from the cave mouth as if it were on fire and suddenly the whole mountain was shaking. Charlie could hear and feel the *THUMP, THUMP, THUMP* of the T. Rex's huge footsteps as it raced from the cave. In an instant

the T. Rex was standing in front of him, his teeth dripping with thick green spit.

Charlie screamed and turned to run in the opposite direction. He could see Steggy's frightened eyes just in front of him.

'Help me!' he shouted to Steggy. 'Do something!'

But it was too late. The T. Rex came thundering towards him and snatched him up in one bony arm. Charlie felt himself being whisked up into the air. He

struggled against the vice-like grip of the T. Rex, but it was hopeless. He turned only to see the mouth of the T. Rex opening high above him. It was filled with a thousand teeth that glinted like spears in the setting sun.

'No!' shouted Charlie as the T. Rex pulled him closer to his mouth. 'No! Please!'

But the T. Rex was too angry to listen. Charlie had invaded his space. Charlie had thrown rocks into his home. Charlie must die. The T. Rex flashed his eyes, opened his mouth wider and pulled Charlie closer.

When the rock hit the T. Rex on the back of the head he froze. Charlie was just moments from death and he could see the T. Rex's tonsils. Another rock hit the T. Rex and the dinosaur turned to look. Steggy was standing a few metres away. He had found a pile of sharp stones and was using his tail to hit them towards the T. Rex one by one. Now that he had the T. Rex's attention, Steggy wiggled his bum at him. The T. Rex's eyes narrowed when he saw the dinopants, and he screeched in rage.

Steggy danced about blowing raspberries and wiggling his bum for all he was worth. If the T. Rex had been angry before, now he was fit to explode. The sight of Steggy in his dinopants seemed to unlock a whole new level of rage in the dinosaur and suddenly

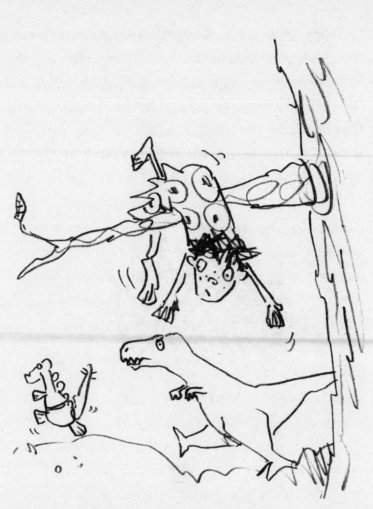

Charlie was forgotten. He threw the boy to one side like a rag doll and lunged at Steggy. Charlie flew through the air and landed in the branches of a tree.

'Oof!' he went, as he was winded by a branch. He clung on for dear life and pulled himself up to a safe position.

Below him the T. Rex was chasing Steggy round and round in circles. Steggy was dodging this way and that, avoiding the lethal swipe of the T. Rex's claws and the killer swish of his tail. From his position in the tree, Charlie could see exactly what was going on and shouted instructions down to Steggy.

'Dive to the right!' he yelled. 'He's just behind you.'

Having got the T. Rex's attention, Steggy didn't know what to do with it – he hadn't thought that far ahead, he only knew that he had to save his friend. Now, as he dodged this way and that, he hoped the T. Rex would tire before he did.

'That's it, Steggy!' called Charlie, seeing his plan. 'Just keep out of his way!'

Steggy waved at his friend. He was winning. He wiggled his pants again at the T. Rex before darting through his legs.

The T. Rex was getting angrier by the second. Charlie knew that dinosaurs couldn't breathe fire, but the T. Rex looked as if he was about to start trying.

Then something terrible happened. Steggy suddenly tripped on a boulder and flew through the air. Charlie watched him as if he moved in slow motion. Steggy somersaulted once, twice, and then came to rest with a thud in a crumpled heap on the stony ground.

'Steggy!' shrieked Charlie. 'Steggy! You've got to get up!'

But Steggy's eyes were closed.

The T. Rex advanced towards Steggy, an evil smile playing on his fang-filled mouth. He growled a low, rumbling chuckle and bent down to pick up the limp dinosaur.

'Leave him alone, you bully!' shouted Charlie from the tree. 'It's me you want, not him.'

But the T. Rex knew that there was plenty of time to sort out the annoying caveboy after he'd got rid of the meddling dinosaur *and* his dinopants.

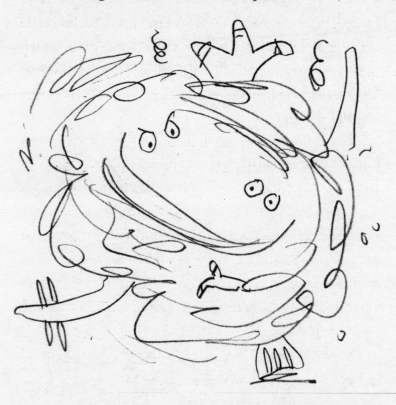

As the T. Rex bent down to pick up Steggy, Steggy's eyes slowly opened. He was dizzy and dazed but he could feel the sharp claws of the T. Rex clutching at his throat. With all his strength, Steggy pushed himself off the ground. He took the T. Rex by surprise and knocked him sideways. The T. Rex fell and tumbled – but he grabbed Steggy with him. Dust and rocks flew everywhere as the dinosaurs wrestled on the ground in a flurry of bites and lashes and growls. The two were locked together and moved so fast that Charlie could no longer tell which eye or tail belonged to which dinosaur. But one thing was clear: as they fought, Charlie watched them getting closer and closer to the edge of the cliff.

'Look out!' he cried, but the dinosaurs were too busy fighting to listen. They scraped and scratched, bit and tore, until in a fury of scales and dust they suddenly tumbled over the side of the mountain.

'Steggy!' shrieked Charlie in despair. 'Steggy!'

But it was too late. Steggy and the T. Rex were gone.

CHAPTER 12

Charlie climbed down the tree and ran to the side of the mountain.

'Steggy!' he called. 'Steggy! Are you all right?'

There was no reply. Charlie hadn't been expecting one. Steggy and the T. Rex had rolled off the cliff to their deaths. There was no way anything was going to survive the huge drop to the bottom. Charlie looked at the scuffed earth where the T. Rex and Steggy had been fighting and shook his head sadly. *Steggy sacrificed himself for me*, he thought. *He shouldn't even have been here. If it wasn't for me and my dinopants none of this would have happened!*

Charlie thumped himself on the arm in anger and then sat down on a rock to cry.

It was then that Charlie heard the noise. He swung round to look at the cave mouth, but there was nothing there. He listened again. The noise was a faint, panting cry, like a baby's whimper and it was coming from the side of the mountain – the side where Steggy and the T. Rex had fallen.

Charlie got up off the rock and tiptoed over.

'Hello?' he called. 'Is there someone there?'

The whimper came again and, excitedly, Charlie crept closer to the cliff edge. His heart was beating fast now. He got down on to his hands and knees and crawled towards the edge. When he was close enough, he lay flat out on his belly and pulled himself to the edge so that he could peer over. Charlie Flint could hardly believe his eyes! 'Steggy!' he cried. 'You're alive!'

Steggy was hanging from a branch about a metre over the edge. His dinopants had snagged themselves on the branch as he had fallen past, and now he was dangling from it like a bouncy dinosaur mobile. And clinging on to one of his legs was the T. Rex.

'No way!' said Charlie. 'My dinopants saved your life!'

Steggy tried his best to smile but it is difficult to be truly happy when you are dangling off a mountainside with a T. Rex.

'*Both* of your lives!' called Charlie to the T. Rex, who growled grumpily.

Charlie had to do something. He couldn't leave Steggy dangling there for ever. The T. Rex must be very heavy – the branch might snap at any time and both of them would find themselves hurtling to the ground.

'Hang on!' he called down to the stranded pair. 'I'm going to get you up.'

But how? He wasn't strong enough to pull two dinosaurs up a cliff face, even if he could reach them. Then Charlie had an idea. But first he needed to sort something out.

'Hey, T. Rex!' Charlie called.

The T. Rex looked up.

'*If* I'm going to rescue you,' said Charlie, 'and it's a big *if*, you have to promise not to eat me or Steggy.'

The T. Rex looked up at Charlie. He seemed to understand what the caveboy was saying and slowly he nodded his head.

'*And*,' continued Charlie, 'you have to stop being such a big bully to all the other dinosaurs. If they want to wear their dinopants you have to let them, OK?'

The T. Rex
snorted angrily and
shook his head.
'Fine,' said Charlie.
'Suit yourself!' And
he got up to walk
away.
Just then, the
T. Rex's grip slipped a
little off Steggy's leg,
and he slid a fraction
closer to his death. He
whined like a startled
horse and began to
growl and screech
frantically.

'Does this mean they can wear their dinopants?' asked Charlie returning to the cliff edge.

The T. Rex nodded until it looked like his head might fly off his shoulders.

'Good,' said Charlie. 'Now wait there. Not that you've got much choice!'

Charlie ran to the cave mouth and scrambled up the side to where the long vines were dangling. Taking a piece of flint from his bag, he hacked off the longest, strongest-looking vine. Then he ran back to the side of the mountain and peered over the edge.

'Are you still there?' he asked.

The two dinosaurs looked up at him. They were panicking now. The T. Rex's grip was getting weaker by the second and it looked like the branch was about to bend to the point of breaking.

'Good,' called Charlie. 'I'm going to lower down a vine. Grab on to it and pull yourselves up.'

Charlie tied one end of the vine to the trunk of the tree, making sure that the knot was good and tight, and then he lowered the other end over the side of the mountain.

'Come on!' he called to the dinosaurs. 'That branch isn't going to last for ever.'

Steggy nudged the vine to the T. Rex, who gripped it tightly with his claws. Then the T. Rex began to pull

himself up the side of the mountain, scrabbling at the loose rock with his feet.

'That's it!' called Charlie in encouragement. 'Nearly there!'

The T. Rex pulled himself safely back on to the mountain top, paused for a moment, then reached over the edge and carefully clamped his mouth around Steggy, and lifted him up to safe ground. Then he collapsed, panting in a heap.

After he'd got his breath back, the T. Rex fixed Charlie with a stare and stood up.

'Remember what you promised!' said Charlie, trying not to let his voice falter.

The T. Rex smiled and stomped towards the little caveboy. With a flash of his beady black eyes he bent down and scooped Charlie up.

'Hey!' cried Charlie. 'You promised!'

The T. Rex lifted Charlie up until they were eyeball to eyeball. The T. Rex stared at Charlie for what felt like an age and then he opened his mouth wide.

Steggy leaped to his feet and growled at the T. Rex, but the T. Rex silenced him with a swish of his tail.

'Hey!' called Charlie in panic. 'We're friends, remember?'

But instead of eating him, the T. Rex growled very softly into his ear.

Charlie laughed. The T. Rex's breath on his ear was ticklish. 'I guess that means "Thank you!"' he giggled, as the T. Rex placed him gently back on the ground. The T. Rex nodded and smiled.

That night Charlie and Steggy slept in the cave with the T. Rex and the following morning, when the sun was high in the sky, they said their goodbyes and began the long walk back down through the clouds to Sabreton.

CHAPTER 13

Back in Sabreton, Billy and James were taking it in turns to kick a ball against the wall.

'It's been over a day since Charlie left,' said Billy miserably. 'Do you think he's all right?'

James turned to look at Billy and raised an eyebrow. 'Charlie went up a mountain to talk to a T. Rex,' he said sarcastically, 'and you're asking me if I think he's all right?'

'Yeah.'

'Of course I don't think he's all right, Billy. In fact, I doubt we'll ever see Charlie Flint again!'

'Never see me again, eh?' said Charlie from behind

them. 'That's a shame – I was hoping for a game of football.'

'Charlie!' shouted Billy in surprise. 'You're alive!'

'Of course I'm alive!' said Charlie. 'You didn't think a T. Rex would get the better of me, did you?'

Billy ran over and hugged Charlie in his bear-like arms.

'Be gentle with me,' he giggled. 'The T. Rex didn't kill me but with hugs like that, *you* might!'

'It's good to see you,' said James, picking up the football and running over to join his friends. 'I was sure you'd be dinopoo yourself by now.'

'So I heard,' said Charlie, thumping James on the arm. 'I would be, too, if it hadn't been for Steggy.'

Steggy smiled and showed the two boys the big rip in the back of his dinopants where the branch had poked through.

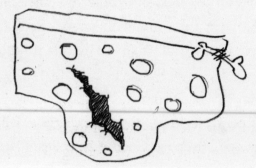

'Charming!' said James with a smile.

The three friends chatted and laughed all the way home as Charlie told them about his adventure on T. Rex's mountain.

By the time he got back to his house, word had spread through Sabreton that Charlie Flint had returned safely from the T. Rex's mountain, and a crowd had gathered by his front door.

Charlie's mum pushed her way through the people. As he opened the gate she ran over and slapped Charlie on the shoulder before smothering him in a big soppy cuddle.

'Don't you *ever* do that to me again!' she said, as she tried to fight back the tears of joy.

'Mum!' whined Charlie, batting her away. 'Don't be so embarrassing!'

But Charlie's mum was having none of it. She was over the moon to see her son alive and didn't care who knew it.

'So what happened, son?' asked Charlie's dad. 'Is it the end of the road for dinopants?'

Charlie laughed and shook his head. 'No way, Dad!' he said. 'It's just the beginning!'

And he stood on his front step and once again told the story of his trip to T. Rex's mountain, about the fight on the cliff top and the exciting rescue. The assembled crowd hung on his every word. Once he had finished, and Steggy had proudly shown off his ripped

dinopants one more time, the crowd clapped and laughed.

'Three cheers for Charlie Flint!' shouted the Mayor, and the crowd joined in enthusiastically.

As the crowds dispersed and Charlie thought the day couldn't get any better, Natalie Honeysuckle came over to him and gave him a kiss on the cheek. 'Well done, Charlie,' she whispered so that only he could hear, and Charlie grinned from ear to ear. Billy and James winked at him.

That night the town held a party in Charlie's honour, and the following day work started once more on the dinopants. Steggy told the other dinosaurs about the T. Rex's promise, and soon they felt confident enough to pull them back on. Before long, every single one of them was proudly wearing a pair again.

A week later, after all the fuss had died down, Charlie crept back to T. Rex's mountain. In the dead of night, while all of Sabreton slept, he took a package from his bag and left it on a rock where he knew the T. Rex would see it. Inside was a pair of special T. Rex dinopants. They were made out of black leather, with his picture across the bum in sparkling studs.

Sometimes, on a clear evening, the people of Sabreton

would look towards the mountain and were just able to see the moonlight reflecting off Charlie's T. Rex dinopants as the proud dinosaur prowled against the night sky.

THE END

piccadillypress.co.uk/children

Go online to discover:

☆ more books you'll love

☆ competitions

☆ sneak peeks inside books

☆ fun activities and downloads